Five reasons why you'll love Isadora Moon . . .

Meet the magical, fang-tastic Isadora Moon!

Isadora's cuddly toy, Pink Rabbit, has been magicked to life!

What would your dream pet be?

Isadora's family is crazy!

Enchanting pink and black pictures

What would your dream pet be?

A sausage dog with a yellow coat called Millie.
– Phoebe

A flying horse because it could take me anywhere.
– Mia

A snow hedgehog because they're very cute.
– Hope

A magic fluffy unicorn
that I can fly on!
– Lola

A pink otter with
invisibility powers.
– Madeleine

A ninja guinea pig!
– Harry

A uni-rabbit, a rabbit
with wings and a unicorn
horn that's magic.
– Iris

Family Tree

My Mum
Countess Cordelia
Moon

Baby Honeyblossom

My Dad
Count Bartholomew
Moon

Me!
Isadora Moon

Pink Rabbit

For vampires, fairies and humans everywhere!

And for Henry, the love of my life.

OXFORD
UNIVERSITY PRESS

Great Clarendon Street, Oxford OX2 6DP

Oxford University Press is a department of the University of Oxford.
It furthers the University's objective of excellence in research, scholarship, and
education by publishing worldwide. Oxford is a registered trade mark of Oxford
University Press in the UK and in certain other countries

British Library Cataloguing in Publication Data

Data available

ISBN: 978-0-19-275851-4

7 9 10 8

Printed in Great Britain by Bell and Bain Ltd, Glasgow

Paper used in the production of this book is a natural,
recyclable product made from wood grown in sustainable forests.
The manufacturing process conforms to the environmental
regulations of the country of origin.

MIX
Paper from
responsible sources
FSC® C007785

ISADORA · MOON

Gets in Trouble

Harriet Muncaster

OXFORD
UNIVERSITY PRESS

Chapter ONE

It was Sunday afternoon and I was hopping up and down with excitement by the kitchen window. My witch fairy cousin Mirabelle was coming to stay! For a whole week!

'It's been ages since we last saw her,'
said Mum, who was busy baking a cake
especially for Mirabelle's arrival.
She was using her wand to stir the
mixture and little sparks kept shooting
out of the bowl.

'I know,' I said. 'I've thought of some good games we can play with the doll's house this time!'

'Lovely!' said Mum.

Suddenly Pink Rabbit started bouncing up and down on the kitchen counter and pointing his paw towards the window. Pink Rabbit used to be my favourite stuffed toy so my mum magicked him alive. She can do things like that because she's a fairy.

'She's here!' I yelled. 'Mum! Look!'

Mum stopped stirring for a moment and we watched as Mirabelle swooped down into the front garden on her broomstick. She looked very glamorous.

'I wish I had a broomstick,'
I said wistfully.

Mum gave me a hug.

'Wings are much nicer than
broomsticks,' she said. She put the bowl
of cake mixture down and we both went
outside into the front garden.

'Mirabelle!' I shouted, running towards her and giving her a big, cousinly hug. 'It's so good to see you!'

'It's good to see you too!' cried Mirabelle, hugging me back. She was wearing a pointy black hat and a pair of shiny lace-up boots, which looked very fashionable.

'Where's Uncle Bartholomew?' asked Mirabelle as we made our way up the stairs towards my turret bedroom.

'Oh, he'll be asleep still,' I told her. 'Remember, Dad always sleeps through the day. He can't bear the sunlight. He'll be up at seven o'clock in the evening for breakfast!'

But just then I heard a clattering
coming from the landing above and Dad
whooshed down the stairs towards us, his
vampire cape billowing out behind him.

'Ah!' he cried. 'My favourite niece!'

'Hello, Uncle Bartholomew,'
said Mirabelle. 'I like
your cape!'

'Well, thank you,' beamed Dad. 'It's pure velvet you know!' Dad loves to get compliments. Vampires are very keen on grooming.

'Come on, Mirabelle,' I said, pulling her past Dad and up the last flight of stairs. 'I've got something to show you.'

'Ta da!' I said as I opened the door. In the middle of my room sat the doll's house. I had covered it with fairy lights. 'And look!' I pointed at the miniature dining room. 'I've set up a welcome tea party for you!'

Inside the tiny room there was a tiny table, and on the tiny table there was a tiny feast.

soft scoop
ice cream

'All the food is real,' I said proudly. 'Even the teeny tiny sandwiches. They took me ages to make. And look! The sweets are made from cake sprinkles!'

Mirabelle gasped. She picked up one of the sandwiches and popped it into her mouth.

'Peanut butter!' she said, 'My favourite!'

'Mine too!' I said happily.

We sat down and ate the food together while Pink Rabbit bounced round the room. He was excited that Mirabelle was here too.

'I'll go and fill up the pool with water,' I said, brushing crumbs off my dress.

Last time Mirabelle came, we'd made
a swimming pool for the dolls out of
an ice cream tub and a waterslide from
plastic tubes stuck together. The slide
was attached to the roof of the house and
twirled all the way down into the pool.
I hurried out of the room to the bathroom
and came back with the ice cream tub
slopping with water.

'I also had another idea,' I said as I put the tub at the bottom of the slide. 'I thought we could make some dolls that look exactly like us! A Mirabelle doll and an Isadora doll, to live in the house and go down the slide! I have loads of scraps of fabric. I think it would be fun. I want my doll to be wearing a black tutu.'

'Hmm,' said Mirabelle. Her eyes suddenly sparkled mischievously. I could tell she was having one of her 'ideas'.

'I've got a better plan,' she said. 'Playing *with* the dolls is boring. Let's *be* the dolls!'

'What do you mean?' I asked.

'Let's shrink ourselves!' said Mirabelle.

'I'll make a potion. Then we can go inside the doll's house and slide down the slide ourselves! It will be so fun!'

She got out her little travelling cauldron from her suitcase and started to pour things into it from tiny glass bottles.

I watched and waited, feeling excited and nervous all at the same time.

'Are you sure nothing will go wrong?'
I said.

'Of course it won't!' said Mirabelle.
She tipped a jar of pink glitter into the
cauldron and stirred. I peered in. It wasn't a
liquid potion but a powdery one. Mirabelle
rummaged in her suitcase again and pulled
out a fluffy powder puff from her washbag.

'Now let me just dab a little bit onto
your arm,' she said. 'A small bit will only
last twenty minutes or so.'

I held out my arm and Mirabelle
dabbed some of the powder onto it with
the puff.

I sat there and waited. All of a sudden
I felt a tingling in my fingers and then . . .

POOF!

There was a cloud of pink glittery
smoke and I landed with a soft thump on
the squashy carpet. I was tiny! Mirabelle
towered over me like a giant.

'Come on!' I shouted up at her in a high, squeaky voice. 'It's your turn!'

Mirabelle burst out laughing.

'Your voice!' she shrieked. 'You sound like a mouse!' She rocked forwards and backwards, laughing until her stomach hurt.

'OK, OK,' she said. 'My turn.' She dabbed some of the powder onto her own arm and there was another POOF of pink, glittery smoke.

'Here I am,' she squeaked, suddenly appearing next to me. 'Look how tiny we are!'

Together we made our way into the doll's house and up the stairs.

We were almost at the roof when we heard a loud thumping sound coming from outside the house.

'What's that?' I whispered, grabbing onto Mirabelle's arm. 'There's something outside!'

We peered out of the window and I breathed a sigh of relief.

'It's just Pink Rabbit!' I said. 'Bouncing around. Poor Pink Rabbit— he didn't see us make the potion. He's probably wondering where we are!'

Pink Rabbit was indeed looking very confused. He was hopping round and round the travelling cauldron blinking his beady button eyes worriedly.

soft scoop
ice cream

I leaned out of the doll's house.

'Pink Rabbit!' I called in my high, squeaky voice. 'Over here!'

Pink Rabbit looked up and saw me. He waggled his ears in surprise. Then, before I could say anything else, he jumped right into the cauldron, completely covering himself with the powdery potion. There was a huge POOF of pink, glittery smoke.

'Uh oh . . .' said Mirabelle as we watched the now miniature Pink Rabbit bounce out of the cauldron and across the carpet to the doll's house.

'What?' I said. 'Pink Rabbit won't mind being tiny. He just wanted to join in!'

'It's not that,' said Mirabelle. 'He covered his whole body in the potion. He's going to be tiny for days!'

'Oh . . .' I said, starting to panic.

'Well there's nothing we can do about it,' said Mirabelle as Pink Rabbit came bounding up the stairs and into my arms. 'Let's not worry about it; let's go and have fun!'

The three of us ran up the rest of the stairs and onto the roof of the doll's house, where the top of the slide was.

'This is going to be amazing!' said Mirabelle. 'You go first, Isadora.'

I peered down the slide. It looked very steep and twisty from up here.

The pool at the bottom suddenly seemed very deep. I had only just learned how to swim underwater.

'It's OK,' I said. 'You can go first, Mirabelle.'

Mirabelle's eyes flashed wickedly.

'Don't be a scaredy-cat, Isadora,' she said. 'Go on. I DARE you.'

I put my foot tentatively at the top of the slide.

'But Pink Rabbit hates getting wet,' I pointed out. 'I should probably stay up here with him.'

'Pink Rabbit won't mind,' said Mirabelle. 'He can wait here. Anyway, you've got wings; you can always fly off the slide if you don't like it.'

This was true.

'OK . . .' I said, putting my other
foot onto the slide and sitting down.

I closed my eyes and held my
nose with my fingers.

'One, two, three, GO!'
shouted Mirabelle,
giving me a little
push.

I was off!

'Wheeee!' I squealed as I whooshed downwards, twisting and turning, my hair flying out behind me. Round and round I spiralled until . . .

SPLOSH!

soft scoop
ice cream

I landed in the ice cream tub full of water.

'Wow!' I gasped, coming up for air and spraying water everywhere. 'That *was* amazing!' Just then there was another SPLOSH and Mirabelle came flying off the slide and into the water beside me.

'That was SO fun!' she said. 'Come on, Isadora, let's do it again!'

I grabbed her hand and we flew back up to the roof. Mirabelle went first this time and I followed her. We tried the slide on our fronts and our backs and going down together. Each time we landed with a wonderful SPLOSH in the tub of water.

I was halfway down the slide on my fourth go when I suddenly felt a tingling in my fingers.

Oh no! I thought. But before I could do anything there was a POOF of pink glittery smoke.

'Help!' I shouted as my body switched back to its normal size and I landed with a thump on the carpet, crushing the whole slide beneath me. Quickly I picked Mirabelle and Pink Rabbit off the roof of the doll's house and set them down on the carpet. There was another POOF and Mirabelle appeared, full size, standing beside me. Pink Rabbit was still the size of a button. I picked him up so he could sit on my hand.

'The poor slide,' I said sadly, staring at it, crushed next to the doll's house. 'We should have been more careful with the potion.'

'You worry too much,' said Mirabelle. 'We can always make another one.'

'I know,' I said. 'But I'm sad it's broken.'

Just then I heard Mum calling us from downstairs.

'Isadoooora! Mirabelle! Breakfast time!'

I looked down at my hand where tiny Pink Rabbit was bouncing up and down. I couldn't let Mum and Dad see him in that state. Carefully I placed him on the bed.

'You have a nap, Pink Rabbit,' I said
to him. 'Hopefully you'll be the right size
when we get back!'

Chapter TWO

Mirabelle and I ran down the stairs and into the kitchen where Mum, Dad, and my little sister, Baby Honeyblossom, were waiting to start our evening breakfast. There was a big cake with pink icing in the middle of the table, made especially for Mirabelle.

'There you are!' said Mum.

'You look wet,' remarked Dad, glancing worriedly towards the window. 'Is it raining? I do hope not. I can't bear getting my hair messed up when I go for my nightly fly.'

'It's not raining,' said Mum, looking at us questioningly. She waved her wand so that our clothes magically became dry again.

'Thank goodness for that,' said Dad, taking a sip of his red juice. Dad only ever drinks red juice. It's a vampire thing.

'I hope you two haven't been making a mess upstairs,' said Mum as she started to cut the cake.

'Um . . .' I began thinking about the crushed slide and the water that had got sloshed all over my bedroom floor.

'Of course not!' said Mirabelle sweetly as we sat down at the table together. 'The cake looks delicious, Auntie Cordelia.'

'Thank you,' beamed Mum. 'It's carrot cake.'

'Oh, Pink Rabbit's favourite,' said Dad with a wink.

Pink Rabbit can't really eat food but he likes to pretend.

'Where is Pink Rabbit?' asked Mum, looking around suspiciously. 'It's very unlike him to miss cake.'

I felt my face go hot.

'He's napping,' said Mirabelle quickly.

'Ah, yes,' nodded Dad knowledgeably. 'He's got a big day coming up tomorrow. He needs his beauty sleep.'

'Tomorrow . . .' I said. *What was happening tomorrow?* And then I remembered. It was bring-your-pet-to-school day!

'Don't tell me you've forgotten,' said Dad. 'You've been looking forward to it for weeks!'

'Pink Rabbit's been practising tricks to show the class,' said Mum to Mirabelle proudly. 'He's been getting very good at juggling.'

'But I thought you took Pink Rabbit to school with you every day anyway?' said Mirabelle, confused. 'Your class will have seen him already.'

'Yes,' I said. 'But I promised him he could come as my special pet, and the class won't have seen his tricks!'

'I see,' said Mirabelle, not seeming like she did at all. Her eyes glittered dangerously as she munched on her sandwich.

After breakfast we raced back upstairs to my bedroom. 'Please, please let Pink Rabbit be his normal size again,' I whispered as I opened my door. But Pink Rabbit was still tiny. He was bouncing and sliding up and down the lumps and bumps in my quilt. To him they were like mountains.

'Oh no!' I wailed. 'What if he's still like this tomorrow? I can't bring him in to school. He might get lost!'

'Well . . .' said Mirabelle. 'I've had an idea . . .'

'What idea?' I asked. I was starting to feel a bit wary of Mirabelle's 'ideas'.

'How about taking a different pet into school tomorrow? I could magic you up an amazing pet. Something no one will have seen before, something really cool. Like . . . a dragon! Everyone would be so impressed.'

'Erm . . .' I began.

'Oh, go on,' wheedled Mirabelle. 'Let me do it! It would be awesome!'

'I don't think so,' I said. 'It's too dangerous. What if it set fire to the school?'

'It won't,' promised Mirabelle. 'I would make one that didn't breathe fire, just stars and glitter! Oh, pleeeease let's do it. I could just make a cute little baby one!'

'Well . . . maybe,' I said, starting to feel tempted by the idea. 'Just a little one then.'

That night, after Mum and Honeyblossom were in bed and Dad had gone out for his nightly fly, Mirabelle got out her travelling potion kit again. We sat in the dark and I used my wand as a torch so she could see what she was doing.

Into the cauldron went the ingredients of the spell: a pinch of stardust, a sprinkling

of dragon scales, a dash of glitter, and a
handful of dried flower petals. Mirabelle
said some strange-sounding words and
gave the potion a stir. We both peered in
and watched the mixture twinkle in the
wand light.

'Just wait,' whispered Mirabelle. 'And watch.'

The mixture began to swirl around all on its own. Round and round it went until it had shaped itself into a ball. The ball began to grow a tail and then legs and feet and claws.

'Look at its wings!' breathed Mirabelle.

We both watched as the tiny little dragon took shape.

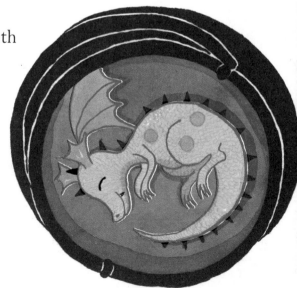

'Oh, it's so cute!' I said.

Mirabelle reached into the cauldron
and stroked it with her hand. The dragon
nuzzled into her finger and squeaked.

'You just need to stroke it,' advised
Mirabelle. 'It's only a baby. It needs to be
comforted.' She picked the dragon up and
put it into my lap. Then she jumped off my
bed and into her own.

'Goodnight, Isadora,' she yawned. Then she lay down, closed her eyes, fell asleep, and started snoring.

I put the dragon carefully under my quilt and then snuggled down next to it in the bed. It felt strange to have the dragon there instead of Pink Rabbit. I had put Pink Rabbit in a little matchbox bed on my bedside table. I didn't want to accidentally roll on top of him in the night when he was so tiny!

I was just dropping off to sleep when . . .

Squeak, squeak, squeak.

I opened one eye.

Squeak! Squeak! Squeak!

The dragon wanted comforting.
I reached out and patted it sleepily on
the head.

'Now you settle down,' I whispered.
'I have school tomorrow!'

The dragon curled up and I lay back down to sleep. My eyes started to close and my mind started to drift away into dreamland when . . .

Squeak, squeak, squeak!

SQUEAK! SQUEAK! SQUEAK!

I sat up in bed.

'Shh!' I whispered, hurriedly patting the dragon on the head again and stroking its little wings. I was worried that it might wake Mum and Honeyblossom.

The dragon stopped squeaking and I lay back down in bed. By the time I finally got to sleep it was way past midnight. I still felt tired when I woke up the next morning.

'Rise and shine, Isadora!' said Mirabelle, leaping up out of bed and looking as fresh as a daisy. 'Where's the dragon?'

I rolled over and peered at her through sleepy eyes.

'What dragon?' I said.

Then I remembered. The dragon!
Immediately I sat bolt upright in bed and
looked around. The dragon had disappeared
from my bed and there was a trail of stars
and glitter running all the way towards my
bedroom door.

Together we followed the trail
downstairs to the kitchen.
'Do you know anything about
this?' Mum asked,

pointing at the glittery, starry floor.

'Well . . .' I began to explain.

'No!' said Mirabelle. 'We don't.

We have been sleeping soundly all night.'
She gave my Mum a sweet smile and sat
down at the breakfast table. I went to sit
next to her but I couldn't relax. I felt guilty
that neither of us had told the truth.

'Evening!' called Dad cheerily as he
came into the house from his nightly fly. 'I
mean, morning, sorry!' I heard him taking
off his cape in the hallway. And then . . .

'What's this?' he asked, coming into
the kitchen and holding his slippers up
with a finger and thumb. Glittery slime
was dripping from the toes.

Oh no! I thought.

'Something's slobbered on my
slippers!' said Dad, horrified. 'I can never

wear these again! I can't possibly wear
slippers that have been slobbered on!
What sort of vampire would that make
me?'

'One that cares about the environment,' said Mum, tapping them with her wand so that the slime disappeared. 'Don't throw them away— that would be very wasteful.'

I heard Mirabelle giggle from behind her toast but I didn't find Dad's slobbered-on slippers very funny. I was too worried about finding the dragon.

Mum stared hard at Mirabelle and me. 'There's something fishy going on,' she said. 'I think you two know something about it.'

'We don't,' insisted Mirabelle. 'Do we, Isadora?'

'Umm,' I said. I didn't want to lie to

Mum but I also didn't want to look bad in front of Mirabelle.

'I think Honeyblossom must have dribbled on Dad's slippers,' I said quickly. 'And I saw her with a packet of sequins yesterday. She must have sprinkled them all over the floor.'

'Yes,' agreed Mirabelle, nodding.

Mum frowned. 'What about Pink Rabbit?' she asked. 'He's missing again.'

'He's in my bedroom,' I said truthfully.

'Getting ready for his big day,' lied Mirabelle. 'He's choosing his best waistcoat to wear!'

'Hmm,' said Mum.

I chewed slowly on my piece of toast but it tasted like cardboard.

'I'm going to go and get ready for school,' I said, hopping off my chair and scuttling out of the kitchen. Where, oh where, could the dragon be? Stars and glitter were everywhere! I searched in the downstairs bathroom, the great hall, the grand dining room, and the sitting room, but the dragon was nowhere to be found.

I made my way back up to my bedroom . . . and there was the dragon! It was sitting curled up on my bed and puffing out clouds of stars and glitter into the air. It was also three times the size it had been last night.

'It's huge!' I wailed to Mirabelle. 'You said it would just be a small one!'

'Well, I meant at first,' explained Mirabelle. 'It's a magic dragon, you see. It will only last for a day and then disappear.' She looked at the clock on my wall. 'It's probably a teenager now.'

'A teenager!' I squeaked. 'I can't take a teenage dragon to school!'

'Of course you can!' insisted Mirabelle. 'All your friends will be amazed!'

'I suppose,' I said, walking to my wardrobe and taking out my school uniform. 'But I wish you were coming too. I don't know how I'm going to look after it on my own.'

'You'll be fine,' said Mirabelle breezily.
'And there's no way I'm coming to school
with you today. Not on my half-term! Just
relax, Isadora.'

'OK,' I sighed, wishing that my school
was on half-term too. Witch schools and
human schools have very different holidays.

I chose to go to a human school even though I am a vampire fairy.

I tried very hard to relax as I put on my school uniform and kissed Pink Rabbit goodbye on the top of his miniature head. When I was ready I got my dressing gown cord and tied it round the dragon's neck to make a lead.

'Now I just have to get the dragon out of the house without Mum and Dad seeing,' I said.

'Easy,' said Mirabelle. 'You can fly out of your bedroom window. It's got wings too, remember! I'll tell your Mum that you were running late for school today and had to rush. I'll tell them that Pink Rabbit was having trouble deciding which waistcoat to wear.'

Pink Rabbit shook his head crossly at Mirabelle from the bedside table.

'No, don't blame it on Pink Rabbit!' I said hurriedly. 'Poor Pink Rabbit!'

I took the end of the dressing gown cord and led the dragon towards the window.

'Goodbye!' said Mirabelle cheerfully
as I stepped out of the window into the air
and flapped my wings. I gave a tug on the
lead and the dragon followed, leaping out
into the morning sunshine. It felt strange
to be without Pink Rabbit and I felt a bit
sad that I hadn't said goodbye to Mum
and Dad but I didn't know what else to do.

Chapter
THREE

Together the dragon and I flew over the
town and towards the school. As we got
closer I could see some of my friends
standing in a group in the playground
with their pets.

'Hey, look!' shouted Oliver, pointing
upwards. 'There's Isadora!'

'Hi Isadora!' called Zoe.

'Wow!!' cried Samantha.

'She's brought a DRAGON!' yelled Sashi.

I landed in the playground with the dragon and everyone immediately began to cluster round.

'That's amazing!' said Jasper.

'Incredible!' agreed Bruno.

'Woah!' said Zoe.

The dragon smiled proudly and puffed out a cloud of stars and glitter. Its scales shimmered in the sunshine. I suddenly felt very pleased that I had brought such an interesting pet into school.

'Do you want to have a ride?' I asked

my friends. 'I'm sure the dragon wouldn't mind.'

'Yes!!' cried Bruno. 'I want a ride. Let me go first!'

He hopped onto the dragon's back and the dragon flew up into the air.

It did a little circle and then landed gently back on the ground.

'Wheee!' squealed Bruno.

'I want a go!' shouted Oliver.

One by one my friends all had a go on the dragon's back until Miss Cherry spotted what was happening and came racing into the playground looking very shocked and surprised.

'What's going on?' she shrieked. 'This is a health and safety hazard! Everyone, come inside immediately!'

The dragon flapped back down to the ground and we all followed Miss Cherry into the classroom.

I sat down at my desk and the dragon

sat next to me. It kept puffing out clouds of stars and glitter into the air. The boy sitting in front of me began to sneeze.

'Now,' said Miss Cherry from the front of the class, 'we are all going to take turns to come up to the front of the class and talk about our pets! Who wants to go first?'

Bruno shot his hand up into the air and Miss Cherry beckoned him to the front.

'This is George the iguana,' said Bruno, holding out a large lizard-like creature for everyone to see. He has a—a—*atishoo!*—a stripy tail and—*atishoo!*—he needs to be kept warm . . .'

'Lovely,' said Miss Cherry. '*Atishoo!*'

Bruno continued talking about his iguana but he was finding it difficult. The air was becoming thick with stars and glitter. It wasn't long before everyone in the classroom was sneezing. Glitter can be very itchy when it gets up your nose!

'Oh dear!' said Miss Cherry through sneezes. 'I think you had better go next, Isadora, and then maybe take the dragon outside for a bit.'

I walked up to the front of the
class. The dragon followed me excitedly,
wagging his scaly tail.

'Um,' I began, feeling a bit shy.
'This is—*atishoo!*—a dragon!'

The dragon hopped up and down
next to me. It started to flap its wings
proudly.

'Dragons like . . . umm . . .'
I continued, realizing that actually
I didn't know much about dragons at all.
'ATISHOO!'

The dragon flapped its wings harder,
disturbing a box of art supplies next to
Miss Cherry's desk. Pencils and crayons
exploded into the air.

'I think—' began Miss Cherry, but at
that moment the dragon knocked over a
row of poster paints, which fell over and
burst open, spattering paint up the walls
and all over the floor.

'Er . . .' I continued, feeling panicked.

The dragon was extremely excited now. It rose up into the air and tried to fly around the room, knocking over anything in its path. Zoe's puppy began to bark and leap across the desks, Samantha's Siamese cat started to yowl, while Jasper's snake hissed and slithered away from him.

'Aargh!' screamed Samantha, jumping up on top of her desk. 'The snake is on the loose!'

Ten seconds later, the classroom was in chaos.

'HEEELP!' shrieked Samantha.

'Where's my snake?' shouted Jasper.

'STOP!' I yelled at the dragon.

But the dragon didn't want to stop. It was enjoying itself too much.

'Oh my goodness!' wailed Miss Cherry with her head in her hands.

I didn't know what to do. The dragon was destroying the classroom. Round and round it went, wrecking everything in its wake. There was nothing else for it . . .

I opened the window.

As soon as the dragon sensed the fresh air it launched itself towards it. *Flap, flap, flap,* went its shimmery scaly wings and my hair blew back in the breeze. Stars and glitter swirled around the room.

And then it was gone. It flew out across the playground and up

into the sky, my dressing gown cord
still tied around its neck. I hoped that
it would fly far away and never come back.

I closed the window quickly so that none of the other pets could escape. Miss Cherry breathed a sigh of relief but she looked very cross.

'Isadora Moon,' she said. 'You are in big trouble.'

I felt my face go red. I had never been in trouble at school before.

'Bringing a dragon to school was an irresponsible thing to do. A dragon is not an appropriate pet for the classroom.'

'I'm sorry,' I said, hanging my head in shame. 'I just—'

'You will be sent home for the rest of the day,' said Miss Cherry. 'Go and see the school secretary now. And you had better spend the afternoon trying to find that dragon!'

I felt like crying as I made my way across the room to the door. Zoe patted my arm gently as I went past her.

'It's OK,' she whispered. 'Miss Cherry will calm down soon.'

'Don't worry,' whispered Bruno.

'I've been sent home before.'

But I had never been sent home from school. I felt so awful. I left the classroom and walked across the lunch hall towards the secretary's office. I knocked on the door.

'Come in,' called a high tinkly voice.

I went into the room and saw Miss Valentino sitting behind the desk wearing her usual pair of pink horn-rimmed glasses.

'What can I do for you, Isadora Moon?' she asked with a beaming smile. 'Have you got another gold star?'

I gulped and felt my eyes prick with tears.

'I've—I've been sent home,' I whispered.

Miss Valentino frowned.

'Oh dear,' she said. 'That's not like you. What happened?'

I explained about Mirabelle and the dragon and Miss Valentino nodded gravely.

'You've got yourself into quite a pickle haven't you?' she said. 'I think it might be time to stand up to that cousin of yours.'

She picked up the phone and dialled my house number.

'Ah, Mrs Moon!' I heard her say. 'It's the secretary from the school here. I'm afraid I must ask you to come and pick Isadora up early today . . . mmm . . . yes . . . yes . . . well, I'll let Isadora explain for herself. OK . . . goodbye, Mrs Moon!' She put the phone down and smiled at me.

'It's all right, Isadora,' she said kindly. 'Everything will be OK.'

It only took Mum ten minutes to appear at the school to fetch me. She must have flown there at top speed.

'What's happened?' she asked as we walked across the playground.

'Why have you been sent home early? And where's Pink Rabbit?'

'I—' I began, 'I—' Suddenly I couldn't bear to tell Mum what had happened.

'I had a tummy ache,' I lied. 'And Zoe is dropping Pink Rabbit home for me later.'

I felt bad about lying and I wasn't
sure Mum would believe me about Pink
Rabbit, but she just nodded her head
and said, 'Poor you. What a shame! We'd
better get you home.' She took my hand
and we both rose up into the air, flapping
our wings.

Chapter FOUR

Mirabelle was in the kitchen when we got back. I saw she had been making moon- and star-shaped cookies with Mum. They must have had a lovely day together.

'Oh, yum,' I said, reaching out to take one.

'Not for you,' said Mum, swiping my hand away gently. 'Not if you have a tummy ache!' She filled a glass with fizzy water for me instead.

'Where's the dragon?' whispered Mirabelle as soon as Mum's back was turned.

'It flew away,' I whispered. 'Shh!'

I spent the rest of the afternoon sitting in the kitchen with Mum and Mirabelle, watching them ice the cookies

and sipping my fizzy water. I popped back up to my bedroom a couple of times to check on Pink Rabbit but he was still tiny.

By breakfast time, Pink Rabbit had still not returned back to his normal size.

'I thought you said Zoe was dropping him off,' said Mum as she put sandwiches and cakes on the table.

'She did,' said Mirabelle quickly. 'Earlier. You were upstairs with Honeyblossom. Pink Rabbit is having a nap—he's tired after his busy day.'

'Pink Rabbit seems to be having a lot of naps lately,' said Dad suspiciously.

'Yes,' agreed Mum, staring at me quizzically. 'He does . . .'

'DELICIOUS sandwiches, Auntie Cordelia!' said Mirabelle in a louder voice than usual. 'Really yummy.'

'Oh, thank you, Mirabelle.' said Mum, delighted. 'They're special fairy ones. They change flavour every time you take a bite.'

'I thought so,' said Mirabelle. 'Mmm! Chocolate spread and raspberry jam!'

I put a sandwich on my plate and nibbled at it. I was feeling worse and worse about all the lies we had been telling to Mum and Dad. If only Pink Rabbit would return to his normal size!

But then I heard something that made my blood run cold. A clanging, crunching, gushing sound coming from upstairs. The sort of sound a dragon might make if it had been let loose in the house . . .

'What on earth is that?' said Mum.

'I have absolutely no idea!' said Dad standing up and swishing his cape around him. 'Let's go and look. Maybe it's a burglar.' He picked up his glass of red juice. 'I shall throw this on the burglar,' he announced. 'It will surprise him.' Mum picked up her wand.

'I think this

might be more useful in this situation,' she said.

Mirabelle picked up her fork and held it in front of her.

'How exciting,' she said. 'I will poke the burglar with my fork!'

We all ran up the stairs to the bathroom.

I tried to get there first but Dad was a lot faster than me with his super speedy vampire cape.

'WHAT'S THIS?!' I heard him gasp as he walked into the room.

The dragon was sitting in the bath and it had half a water pipe in its mouth that it had ripped out from beneath the basin. Water was gushing all over the bathroom floor, and stars and glitter swirled everywhere. Mum waved her wand to stop the water temporarily.

'We'll have to call a plumber tomorrow,' she said. 'to fix it properly.'

Then she narrowed her eyes at me.

'Isadora Moon,' she said in a stern voice. 'I do believe that is your dressing gown cord tied around that dragon's neck.'

I hung my head.

'What HAS been going on?' asked Dad with his hands on his hips. 'I thought you were behaving strangely, Isadora.'

'Very strangely,' agreed Mum. 'All this lying and sneaking around.'

'I'm sorry,' I said in a small voice. Mirabelle stood behind me and said nothing.

'Now answer me honestly,' said Mum. 'Is this Pink Rabbit in the bath? Have you turned him into a dragon? Is this why we haven't seen him lately?'

'No!' giggled Mirabelle. 'That's not Pink Rabbit!'

Mum didn't seem to find it very funny.

'Pink Rabbit is napping,' said Mirabelle again. 'He's—'

But I couldn't bear to tell any more lies.

'He's not napping,' I said to Mum and Dad. 'He's turned into a miniature rabbit.'

'What?!' said Dad.

'We made a potion,' I gabbled, 'and Pink Rabbit jumped into it and is now really tiny. And I crushed my doll's house slide when I grew big again and then we made another potion so that I would have a really interesting pet to take to school. A dragon. But the dragon just made a mess everywhere so I blamed it on Honeyblossom. Then it got me into trouble at school and I was sent home ... but the dragon had flown away so I told you I had a tummy ache ... I'm sorry.'

'I see,' said Dad, looking
disappointed. Mum shook her head and I
started to cry. Mirabelle stood there, not
saying a word.

'You are grounded for a week,' said Dad. 'Literally. No more flying. No more magic and no more peanut butter sandwiches!'

'Yes,' agreed Mum. 'All this lying! What sort of example are you setting to your cousin?'

I sniffed sadly.

Then Mirabelle spoke up. Her face had gone very red.

'Um,' she said, 'it's not all Isadora's fault.' Then she started to explain. 'Really, it's mostly my fault,' she said looking down at the floor. 'I persuaded her to do everything. Isadora didn't want to make the dragon or take it to school.

She wasn't even very keen on making the shrinking potion. I'm sorry too.'

'I see,' said Mum, softening a bit.

'Hmm,' said Dad.

They both turned to me.

'Isadora,' said Mum. 'You need to learn to stand up for yourself.'

'You mustn't ever do things you don't want to do just because someone else wants you to,' said Dad.

'I know,' I said in a small voice.

'And Mirabelle,' said Dad. 'You should know better! You are older than Isadora. We don't want any more mischief this week.'

'OK,' said Mirabelle meekly.

'Well then,' said Mum, brightening up a bit. 'Let's put this behind us.'

'But you're still grounded,' added Dad cheerfully as he took hold of the dressing gown cord and began to lead the dragon out of the bathroom. 'BOTH of you.'

We all went back downstairs with the dragon and finished our breakfast. The dragon must have been very hungry because it ate all of the sandwiches and then gobbled down all the cake. It even drank a glass of Dad's red juice.

'Poor thing,' said Mum.

After breakfast Mirabelle and I went back to my bedroom with the dragon who was now almost the size of a car! Pink Rabbit was there sitting on the bed . . .

And he was normal size!!

'Oh, Pink Rabbit!' I said, hugging him tightly to my chest. 'You're back to yourself again!' Pink Rabbit squirmed happily in my arms and wiggled his ears. The dragon flapped its wings happily.

'It's probably a very old dragon now,' observed Mirabelle, giving its snout a gentle pat. 'Probably about one hundred years old!'

'It seems fidgety,' I said. 'Do you think it needs a fly before bedtime?'

'Maybe,' said Mirabelle, opening the window. 'Shall we go for a last ride on its back before it disappears?'

'I don't know,' I said. 'Dad did say no more flying for a week.'

'Oh yes,' said Mirabelle, a naughty glint flashing in her eyes. 'Well *we* wouldn't really be flying, would we? The dragon would be flying.'

She had a point. I did so want to go for a last fly on the dragon. And not just because Mirabelle wanted to.

'OK,' I agreed. 'Let's go. But I'm going because I want to. Not because you think it's a good idea.'

We both climbed onto the dragon's back and I held Pink Rabbit tightly to my chest. The dragon puffed a cloud of stars and glitter out of its snout happily.

Then it launched itself out of the window
and into the starry sky.

'That was wonderful!' I said, when we got back to my bedroom.

'It was,' agreed Mirabelle.

The dragon yawned and curled up on my floor. Mirabelle and I both got into bed and I turned out the light.

'Goodnight, dragon,' we whispered.

Then next morning, when we woke up, the dragon had gone. There was just a pile of stars and glitter on floor. I felt a tiny bit sad.

'It's OK,' said Mirabelle, patting me gently on the arm. 'I can magic you up another one.'

'No!' I said firmly. 'Absolutely not.'

'But—' said Mirabelle.

'No,' I said.

Then I hopped out of bed and pulled my doll's house into the middle of the floor.

'Let's play my game today,' I said. 'Let's make doll's house characters that look like us after breakfast. I think that would be really fun!'

I got out my box of fabric scraps.

'We don't even need any magic to do it,' I said happily. 'We can make them the old-fashioned way. Mine will have a black tutu.'

'OK,' said Mirabelle, starting to sound excited. 'Can mine have some little pointed black boots?'

'Of course it can,' I said. 'That would look amazing! We can make a tiny Pink Rabbit too.'

Together we went down the stairs to breakfast, Pink Rabbit bounding along behind us.

'You know what *would* be fun,' said Mirabelle, her eyes glinting again. 'If we magicked the dolls alive! We could—'

'No,' I said firmly. 'We're not going to do that, Mirabelle.'

'OK,' said Mirabelle meekly.

'It will be fun anyway. I promise!' I said.

And it was.

Are you more fairy or more vampire?

Take the quiz to find out!

What's your favourite colour?

A. Pink   **B.** Black   **C.** I love them both!

Would you rather go to:

A. A glittery school that teaches magic, ballet, and making flowery crowns?

B. A spooky school that teaches gliding, bat training, and how to have the sleekest hair possible?

C. A school where everyone gets to be totally different and interesting?

On your camping holiday, do you:

A. Put up your tent with a wave of your magic wand and go exploring?

B. Pop up your fold-out four-poster bed and avoid the sun?

C. Splash about in the sea and have a great time?

Results

Mostly As

You are a glittery, dancing fairy and you love nature!

Mostly Bs

You are a sleek, caped vampire and you love the night!

Mostly Cs

You are half fairy, half vampire and totally unique – just like Isadora Moon!

Isadora Moon series

ISADORA MOON

Goes to the Ballet

Half vampire, half fairy, totally unique!
Harriet Muncaster

ISADORA MOON

Gets in Trouble

Half vampire, half fairy, totally unique!
Harriet Muncaster

ISADORA MOON

Goes on a School Trip

Half vampire, half fairy, totally unique!
Harriet Muncaster

Isadora Moon
Goes to School

Her mum is a fairy and her dad is a vampire
and she is a bit of both. She loves the night, bats,
and her black tutu, but she also loves the sunshine,
her magic wand, and Pink Rabbit.

When it's time for Isadora to start school
she's not sure where she belongs—fairy school
or vampire school?

Isadora Moon
Goes to the Ballet

Her mum is a fairy and her dad is a vampire
and she is a bit of both. Isadora loves ballet,
especially when she's wearing her black tutu,
and she can't wait to see a real show at the
theatre with the rest of her class.

But when the curtain rises,
where is Pink Rabbit?

Harriet Muncaster, that's me! I'm the
author and illustrator of Isadora Moon.
Yes really! I love anything teeny tiny,
anything starry, and everything glittery.

Love Isadora Moon?
Why not try these too...